Zoe's Rescue Zoo

The Messy Meerkat

Amelia Cobb

Illustrated by
Sophy Williams

nosy crow

With special thanks to Siobhan Curham

First published in the UK in 2019 by Nosy Crow Ltd
The Crow's Nest, 14 Baden Place
Crosby Row, London SE1 1YW

Nosy Crow and associated logos are trademarks and/or
registered trademarks of Nosy Crow Ltd

A CIP catalogue record for this book will be available from the British Library

Printed and bound in Great Britain by Clays Ltd, Elcograf S.p.A.

Papers used by Nosy Crow are made from wood grown in sustainable forests.

978 1 78800 436 7

www.nosycrow.com

Chapter One
A New Animal Family

Zoe Parker dipped her brush into a pot of bright-yellow paint. The Rescue Zoo was having a special treasure hunt in a couple of days, just before the end of the summer holidays. The treasure hunt had been Zoe's idea, and she was looking forward to having a brilliant day before school started again!

The zoo had just closed for the evening and Zoe and her mum Lucy were on the grass outside the hippo enclosure, making a banner to let people know about the treasure hunt. Zoe added some long golden rays to the smiley sun at the centre of the banner.

"There – it's finished," she said, feeling proud of her work.

COME TO OUR SUMMER TREASURE HUNT! THIS SATURDAY AT 11, the banner said in

bright, colourful letters. As well as the sun,
Zoe had painted cheery pink, red and
orange flowers clambering around the
words.

"It looks lovely, Zoe," Lucy said as she
began packing away the paints. "It was
such a great idea of yours to have a
treasure hunt. Lots of people have bought
tickets for it."

Zoe grinned. She loved it when the
zoo was full of visitors. But Zoe wasn't a
visitor to the Rescue Zoo. She actually

lived there! Her Great-Uncle Horace had started the zoo a long time ago, as a home for any animals who were lost, poorly or didn't have a home. Zoe's mum was the zoo vet, and she and Zoe lived on the edge of the zoo in a cosy little cottage.

Just then, a little mouse lemur scampered over and looked at the banner, his golden eyes gleaming with excitement.

"Hello, Meep." Zoe picked him up and stroked his silky grey fur. Meep was her very best friend and he lived with Zoe and Lucy in their cottage.

A young hippo called Henry

trundled over to the edge of his enclosure and grunted loudly. His grey skin was covered in splotches of mud. Zoe smiled. Henry loved nothing more than taking a mud bath in the lake in the middle of his enclosure – all the hippos loved the mud! Henry grunted again and nodded at the banner. He was telling Zoe how much he liked it. Zoe knew this because she had a special secret – she was able to talk to animals! They understood her and she understood them. But nobody knew, not even her mum or Great-Uncle Horace. So she just smiled at Henry and nodded.

"And what, may I ask, is going on here?"

Zoe turned to see Mr Pinch standing on the red-brick path with his hands on his hips and a frown on his face.

"Uh-oh!" Meep muttered, and hopped on to Zoe's shoulder.

Mr Pinch was the Rescue Zoo manager. He was tall and thin and nearly always grumpy.

"We're making a banner for the summer treasure hunt," Lucy replied as she packed away the last of the paints.

"Well, you're certainly making a mess," Mr Pinch said. "Look!" He pointed to the grass.

"What?" Zoe asked, puzzled.

"Paint!" Mr Pinch snapped.

Zoe moved closer to where he was pointing and spotted a tiny splash of yellow paint on the grass. "But it's only a speck," she said.

Henry the hippo snorted with laughter. Mr Pinch turned and glared at him.

"And look at that messy hippo," he said, shaking his head. "All covered in mud."

"Hippos are supposed to be covered in mud," Zoe said. "It keeps them cool in this hot weather. Are you looking forward to the treasure hunt?" she asked, trying to change the subject.

"No, I am not," Mr Pinch retorted. "Loads of people scrambling about looking for prizes is not my idea of fun." He turned on his heel and marched off.

Meep hopped down from Zoe's shoulder and marched up and down crossly, pretending to be Mr Pinch. Zoe giggled, Meep was very cheeky indeed!

Just then, Mo the hippo keeper walked past with a wheelbarrow full of sand.

"Hi, Zoe. Hi, Lucy," he called.

"Hello, Mo. What are you doing with

that sand?" Zoe called back.

"I'm preparing a new enclosure for some special animals," Mo replied with a grin.

Zoe's tummy fluttered. She loved it when new animals arrived at the Rescue Zoo!

"What kind of animals are they?" she asked.

"You'll have to wait and see!" Mo replied. "Your Great-Uncle Horace wants it to be a surprise. But if your mum says it's OK you can come and help me get the enclosure ready for them."

Zoe looked at Lucy excitedly.

"Go on," Lucy said with a smile. "I'll join you after I've hung up the banner."

Zoe skipped along the footpath after Mo, with Meep scampering along beside her.

"Why do you think he's got all that sand?" she whispered to Meep. "What kind of animal needs sand?"

"Er – a sand hippo?" Meep suggested.

Zoe looked puzzled. "I don't think there's such an animal as a sand hippo."

Meep looked disappointed. "What about a sand panda?"

"Nope." Zoe shook her head.

"How about a sand-wich? I'm starving!" he said, rubbing his tummy.

"You're *always* starving," Zoe giggled. She took a pack of seeds from her pocket and gave Meep a handful.

They followed Mo round to the back of the hippo enclosure, where a new glass-walled enclosure gleamed in the setting sun. The enclosure was full of dirt and sand. A few logs and rocks were dotted about but apart from that the enclosure was empty.

Zoe watched as Mo let himself in and tipped in the sand from the wheelbarrow. Her mind whirred as she tried to work out what kind of animal the enclosure could be for. Sand was usually found in the desert in hot places like Africa. And Mo was the zookeeper who looked after the hippos, which also came from Africa. Zoe quickly thought of other animals that came from Africa. Lions and leopards and elephants and giraffes... But the Rescue Zoo already had enclosures for those animals, and they were much bigger than this one!

All of a sudden Zoe heard a low hum coming from the sky, which became louder and louder.

Around the zoo the sound of animals bellowing, roaring, trumpeting and chirping filled the air.

"Goo! Goo!" Meep chattered, jumping up and down.

Zoe felt like jumping up and down

with excitement too. Goo was Meep's
nickname for her Great-Uncle Horace
and the noise was coming from the
Rescue Zoo helicopter! Zoe spun round
just in time to see the helicopter coming

in to land on the other side of the new
enclosure.

"Great-Uncle Horace!" she
cried, racing round to greet him
as soon as the blades on the
helicopter roof had stopped.
The door to the helicopter
opened and Great-Uncle Horace
clambered from the cockpit. He was

wearing safari clothes and had a pair
of binoculars around his neck. His
bushy white beard was covered in dust.
A beautiful bright-blue bird fluttered
out after him. It was Kiki, the hyacinth
macaw Great-Uncle Horace had rescued
years ago and who was now his constant
companion.

"Zoe!" Great-Uncle Horace cried,
hurrying over to give her a hug. "It's so
lovely to see you."

"You too!" Zoe replied. "Where have
you been? What animal have you
rescued? Can I meet it?"

Great-Uncle Horace chuckled as Kiki
fluttered down to perch on his shoulder.
"One question at a time! I've been to
Botswana, which is in Africa. It was
marvellous. Although we did get caught in

a flash flood, which was most unexpected and brings me to the answer to your final question…" Great-Uncle Horace looked back at the helicopter. "I have on board a family who sadly lost their home in the flood."

A family! Zoe's eyes lit up. Even though it was sad that the mystery animals had lost their home, she was glad they had a safe new home at the Rescue Zoo. But what kind of animals were they?

Mo came striding over from the new enclosure. "Welcome back, Horace," he called.

"Ah, Mo," Great-Uncle Horace said. "Just the person I need. Would you help me carry our new arrivals to their new home?"

"Of course."

Zoe watched as Mo and Great-Uncle Horace got back on the helicopter and re-emerged carrying a large wooden crate.

"I can't wait to see what's inside," she whispered to Meep.

"Me too!" Meep chirped, jumping up and down.

They followed Great-Uncle Horace and Mo over to the new enclosure.

"Could you open the gate, please, Zoe?" Mo called.

"Of course." Zoe felt for the silver paw-print pendant around her neck. It had been a special gift from Great-Uncle Horace and it opened all of the enclosures in the zoo. She pressed the pendant to a pad next to the gate and it swung open. Mo and Great-Uncle Horace took the crate inside and placed it down in the middle of the sand and dirt. Zoe followed them in with Meep on her shoulder, closing the gate behind her.

"And now, all shall be revealed," Great-Uncle Horace said grandly, before unlocking the lid of the crate and lifting it open. A pointy little face peered over the edge, followed by another and another. The creatures' fur was pale brown, with large black patches around their eyes. Zoe's heart thumped with excitement.

"Are they meerkats?" she smiled.

"They certainly are," Great-Uncle Horace replied, as the three meerkats scrambled from the crate. The larger two stood still and gazed around the enclosure but the smaller one scampered over to the glass wall and looked outside.

"Three meerkats!" Zoe exclaimed.

"Not three," Great-Uncle Horace replied with a grin as he leaned into the crate. "Six." One by one, he gently placed three baby meerkats on the sand. Their fur was paler and fluffier than the others, making them look a bit like puppies.

"Aw, they're so cute!" Zoe exclaimed as the baby meerkats started rolling around on the floor, play-fighting with each other.

"These are the babies – two girls and one boy – and that one over there is their big brother." Great-Uncle Horace pointed to the meerkat looking out of the glass enclosure.

"They're gorgeous!" Zoe cried. "Can I go and get Mum so she can meet them?"

"Of course," Great-Uncle Horace replied.

Zoe hurried back over to the gate and opened it with her pendant. But before she had a chance to leave, a blur of pale-brown fur raced past her and outside. Zoe's stomach lurched. The bigger meerkat pup had escaped!

Chapter Two
The False Alarm

Zoe raced after the pup with Meep right behind her.

"Come back!" she cried. Thankfully the zoo was now closed so the paths were empty. The meerkat scampered past the hippo enclosure, where Lucy had just finished hanging the banner on the fence.

"Where are you off to in such a hurry?"

Lucy called when she saw Zoe running past.

"A meerkat's escaped," Zoe gasped.

"A meerkat?" Lucy looked puzzled. "But we don't have any meerkats."

"We do now!" Zoe cried. "Great-Uncle Horace brought them back with him!"

Zoe ran past the giraffe enclosure, where Jamie the youngest giraffe was grazing by the fence. When he saw Zoe he bleated loudly.

"I can't explain now," Zoe replied breathlessly. "I'm trying to catch a meerkat." Jamie raised his long neck and giggled loudly.

Up ahead of her on the path, the meerkat darted under a large bush outside the panda enclosure.

Zoe ran up to the bush. She heard a

scrambling sound and then the meerkat appeared. His pale-brown fur was covered in dirt and two leaves were stuck on his head.

"Please don't run away again," Zoe panted.

The meerkat stood on his hind legs and looked at Zoe. Then he made a little chattering sound.

"What were you doing then, if you weren't running away?" Zoe said.

The meerkat chattered some more.

"What did he say?" Meep asked, scampering over.

"He was looking for fun," Zoe explained.

Meep giggled. "Fun's a good thing to look for."

The meerkat nodded and a couple of

leaves fell from his head on to the floor. Then he looked around him and yelped.

"You're at the Rescue Zoo," Zoe explained. "My name's Zoe and this is Meep. We live at the zoo with my mum, Lucy. She's the zoo vet. What's your name?"

The meerkat gave a little yelp.

"Welcome to the Rescue Zoo, Max," Zoe replied. "Now, we'd better get you back to your family or they're going to be worried." Zoe gently picked up the meerkat pup. He was very fluffy and didn't weigh very much at all! He seemed to like being held, and climbed up Zoe's arm until his head was peeping over her shoulder. The three friends set off back along the path.

When they got to the new enclosure

Lucy was there, talking to Great-Uncle Horace and Mo.

"Oh thank goodness!" Great-Uncle Horace exclaimed, as Zoe let herself back inside. "I was just about to send out a search party."

"It's OK, he hadn't gone far." Zoe placed Max on the sand next to his parents. They both barked at him, telling him off for running away. Max sighed before going over to join his baby siblings.

"Right, I'd better get these guys settled in for the night," Mo said.

"Can I help?" Zoe asked eagerly.

"It's time for dinner now, Zoe," Lucy said. "And we both need to get an early night. We've got a very busy day ahead of us tomorrow, preparing for the treasure hunt."

"Why don't you come back first thing in the morning?" Mo said to Zoe. "You can help me get the enclosure finished."

"Great, thank you!" Zoe went over to Max and stroked him on the head. "See you tomorrow, Max," she whispered.

Max chattered in her ear and Zoe giggled. "Yes, I'll make sure we do something fun together!"

The next morning Zoe set off bright and early for the meerkat enclosure, with Meep on her shoulder. The sun was just rising and the zoo was still closed. In their enclosures the animals were all starting to wake up.

"I can't wait to see Max and his family again," said Zoe.

"Me too," Meep chirped.

When they got to the new enclosure the meerkat family were standing in a line on one of the logs. Mo was standing outside watching them.

"What are they doing?" Zoe asked.

"Warming up," Mo replied.

"How?" Zoe asked. "They're standing still."

Mo smiled. "See how they're all facing the sun?"

Zoe turned and saw the sun coming up over the hippo enclosure, its golden rays shimmering in the lake. Then she looked back at the meerkats. Mo was right. They were all standing facing the sun!

"Meerkats have patches on their tummies where the fur is a lot thinner," Mo explained. "Every morning when they wake up, they stand like that, facing their tummies to the sun. The heat goes through the patch and warms their whole bodies."

"Kind of like solar panels?" Zoe asked.

Mo laughed. "Yes, kind of like solar panels."

"That's so cool!" Zoe exclaimed.

When Max saw Zoe and Meep he got down from the log and came scampering over, chattering loudly.

"Can you help me bring these logs into the enclosure?" Mo asked, pointing to a pile of logs beside the gate.

"Of course." Zoe picked up one of the logs and followed Mo inside. "What are they for?"

"The meerkats will use them as lookout posts," Mo explained. "When they forage for food or burrow new tunnels one of them always stands guard in case a predator appears."

"But no predators will hurt the meerkats here at the Rescue Zoo," Zoe said.

"No, but the meerkats don't know that!" Mo smiled.

Zoe helped Mo arrange the logs in the enclosure, with Max and Meep scampering around excitedly.

When they finished, the other meerkats jumped down from the log and Max's parents called him over. Zoe went a bit closer so she could hear what they were saying. They were telling Max that they wanted him to teach his baby brother and sisters how to burrow.

Max let out an excited shriek and began digging really fast, sending clouds of sand into the air.

"Meerkats are able to close their ears so the dirt doesn't get into them when they're burrowing," Mo said.

"I wish I could close my ears when Mr Pinch starts grumbling," Meep chirped on Zoe's shoulder, making her giggle.

Max carried on burrowing faster and faster and the cloud of sand grew bigger and bigger. His baby brother and sisters scampered over and started trying to copy him. In seconds they were covered in sand and started to sneeze.

"Oh dear, it's a shame they're not able to close their noses too," Mo chuckled.

Max's mum let out a loud bark to tell Max to stop digging. He emerged from the hole covered in dirt.

Max's dad chattered to him, telling him that was enough burrowing and that he was to stand guard instead. Max clambered on to a rock and stood up straight. Then he gave a big yawn. He didn't look very interested in his new job.

"I'm just going to go and get some more rocks," Mo said, fetching his wheelbarrow from the shed at the side of the enclosure.

"OK! I'll stay here with the meerkats," Zoe replied. Zoe wanted to be a zookeeper when she grew up, so she loved helping out whenever she could – and spending time with the animals was her favourite thing to do!

Once Mo had gone, Zoe watched as Max's parents began teaching the baby meerkats how to burrow. Max stood guard on the rock.

"I don't think he enjoys standing guard," said Meep, as Max let out another giant yawn.

"I know," Zoe replied. "Maybe we should go over and keep him company."

But before they could move Max started yelping really loudly.

"What's he doing?" Meep asked.

"I don't know." Zoe looked around to see what could be making Max bark. But, apart from a few zookeepers finishing their morning jobs, no one was around.

Max's mum and dad gathered the babies together and raced inside a burrow beside one of the logs.

Max ran over to Zoe.

"Where have they gone?" Zoe asked. "And shouldn't you go with them?"

Max chattered his reply.

"Oh! What are they hiding from?" Zoe asked.

Max yelped.

"An eagle?" Zoe looked up into the clear blue sky. It was totally empty apart from a couple of fluffy white clouds. "But there's no eagle up there!"

Max chattered some more.

"Oh dear," Zoe said.

"What's wrong?" Meep asked.

"He said he was bored so he decided to practise his warning bark. He didn't mean for it to be so loud."

Meep chuckled. "He's a very cheeky meerkat!"

Zoe noticed that the little meerkat looked a bit sad. "Don't worry," she said. "I'll go and tell them it's OK." She went over to the entrance of the burrow and called out softly. "It's all right, you can come out now. It was a false alarm."

One by one, the meerkats emerged from the tunnel. Max scampered back on to the rock and the others started burrowing again.

Max chattered to Zoe as he stood guard.

"There are plenty of fun things to do here at the Rescue Zoo – that don't involve scaring your family," Zoe said. "We're having a treasure hunt here on Saturday and that's going to be *loads* of fun." She smiled as she watched Max shake the dirt from his fur. Something told her life certainly wasn't going to be dull with this messy little meerkat around!

Chapter Three
Babies in a Burrow

The next morning Zoe's friend Nicola was coming to spend the day at the zoo. Zoe was really excited as Nicola had been away for most of the summer holiday so she hadn't seen her for ages.

"I'll have to take her to see the meerkats and show her the banners for the treasure hunt," Zoe said to her mum as she sliced some banana for Meep's breakfast. "And then we can check the treasure-hunt map and start writing the clues and go and get ice creams from the café and look around the gift shop and feed the elephants and pet the goats and—"

"Slow down." Lucy laughed. "If you're not careful poor Nicola will be so tired after her day at the zoo she'll need another holiday!"

Zoe grinned. "Well, I'm definitely going to take her to see the meerkats." She put Meep's breakfast bowl on the table and Meep pounced on it hungrily. "Mum, do you think Mo would let us bring one of the meerkats back to the cottage for a while?" Last night, when she'd been trying to get to sleep, Zoe had been thinking of ways to make things fun for Max.

"I don't see why not," Lucy replied as she put a plate of hot buttered toast on the table. "But check with Mo first and if he says yes then make sure he gives you a travel basket to carry the meerkat in. And you'll have to look after him properly; we don't want any more runaway meerkats! And I'll be here at lunchtime to see how you're getting on."

Zoe nodded and grinned. "OK. Thanks, Mum."

As soon as Nicola arrived and Lucy had gone to work, the girls set off for the meerkat enclosure with Meep perched on Zoe's shoulder.

"I can't wait to see the meerkats," Nicola said excitedly. "They're my favourite animal in the whole world!"

Zoe was excited to see the meerkats again too, but as soon as they got to the enclosure her heart sank. Max's dad was barking crossly.

"Uh-oh," Meep chirped in Zoe's ear. "I think Max might be in trouble again!"

Zoe looked through the glass wall of the enclosure. Max was standing by one of the logs, his fur covered in dirt and sand. His dad was standing on top of the log barking at him. There was a huge mound of sand in the centre of the enclosure and Max's mum was crouching beside it, making a sad chirping sound. There was no sign of the babies.

"Ah, look at that little meerkat with all the dirt on his fur!" Nicola cried, pointing at Max. "He's so sweet."

"Good morning, Zoe!" Mo called as he

came out of the shed beside the enclosure.

"Good morning, Mo," Zoe replied. "This is my friend Nicola. She's come to visit for the day. Is it OK if she comes in to see the meerkats with me?"

"Of course," Mo replied. "I'm just going to give the hippos their breakfast. I'll be back soon."

Using her special paw-print pendant, Zoe opened the gate to the enclosure and they went inside. She needed to find out why Max was in trouble again but it was going to be hard to talk to him with Nicola there.

"I wonder why that meerkat is making that noise," Nicola said, pointing to Max's dad, who was still barking.

Zoe moved closer so she could hear him properly. Max was being told off for digging a new twisty-turning tunnel that went round and round in circles. The baby meerkats had gone into it and they were having so much fun they wouldn't come out again!

As Nicola went over to see what Max's mum was doing, Zoe crouched beside him.

Max gave a little yelp.

"I know you didn't mean for them to follow you into the burrow," Zoe whispered, stroking the top of his head. "But can you think of a way to get them to come back out again?"

Max tilted his head to one side thoughtfully, then he grinned and scampered over to the burrow entrance. He started barking softly.

"What's he doing?" Nicola asked.

"I think he's calling to his baby brother and sisters," Zoe replied. She held her breath and watched the entrance to the burrow. She really hoped Max's plan would work! There was a scuffling sound and then a tiny pointy nose appeared in the entrance to the burrow, followed by another, and another.

"Aww, look at the babies!" Nicola cried as they emerged from the burrow. Their fluffy pale fur was covered in dirt.

When the babies saw Max they chattered and started rolling around on the ground. His twisty tunnel had got them all overexcited!

Max's mum nuzzled the babies and Max's dad yelped contentedly. Max looked much happier.

When Mo got back from feeding the hippos, Zoe asked him if she and Nicola could take Max to the cottage for a while.

"I think that's a great idea," Mo said. "Let me go and get something for you."

"He's probably going to get a travel basket for us to carry him in," Zoe said to Nicola as they watched Mo go over to the shed by the enclosure. But to her surprise Mo came back with a collar and lead.

"This little guy is so confident and friendly, I'm going to use him in my demonstrations," Mo explained, as he carefully placed the collar around Max's neck. "It'll be great to get him used to being on a lead."

The little meerkat hopped about with excitement. Zoe felt like hopping about with excitement too. She couldn't believe she was going to be taking a meerkat for a walk!

"Make sure you keep the lead on at all times when you're outside and don't let him eat anything," Mo said as he handed the lead to Zoe.

"OK!" Zoe wrapped the end of the lead

round her hand tightly.

"You're so lucky, Zoe." Nicola smiled
as they began making their way along
the red-brick path past the different
enclosures. "It must be so much fun living
in a zoo."

"It *is* loads of fun," Zoe replied. She
looked down at Max. He certainly
seemed to be having fun too now he was
out of his enclosure – looking at all the
different animals and tugging on his lead.

Just as they were passing the elephants
Mr Pinch appeared, marching up the path
towards them. A frown spread across his
face when he saw Max.

"What is this animal doing out of his
enclosure?" he said crossly.

"We're just taking him for a walk," Zoe
replied.

"Taking him for a walk?" Mr Pinch spluttered.

"Yes. We're going back to the cottage for lunch and to finish the map for the treasure hunt," Zoe said.

Mr Pinch sighed. "I don't know what this zoo is coming too," he grumbled. "Meerkats on leads and treasure hunts!"

The Messy Meerkat

"He was a bit grumpy," Nicola said as soon as Mr Pinch was out of earshot.

"He always is," Zoe replied with a grin. "Although sometimes he can be quite nice."

She opened the door to the cottage and they stepped inside.

"Hello, girls," Lucy called from the kitchen. "Come on through. Your lunch is ready."

While Zoe and Nicola tucked into a lunch of cheese sandwiches and cupcakes, and Meep tucked into a bowl of blueberries, Zoe put Max in the back garden, attaching the end of his lead to the pole of the washing line. She was so pleased that the little meerkat was having fun and really seemed to be enjoying his adventure!

Once they'd finished lunch and Lucy had gone back to work, Zoe fetched her paint set. Lucy had left the treasure-hunt map on the dining-room table for the girls to colour in.

"I'll just go and check on Max," Zoe said, as Nicola started sorting through the paintbrushes.

Meep scampered after Zoe as she went through to the back garden.

"Uh-oh!" Meep chirped.

"Oh no!" Zoe exclaimed.

Max was grinning happily on top of a huge heap of earth where one of the flowerbeds used to be. The grass beside him was littered with uprooted flowers and he had a pansy stuck behind one of his ears.

Max scampered over and chattered

excitedly to Zoe.

"Oh, Max," she sighed. "I'm sure you have dug a lovely burrow, but I'm not sure what Mum's going to say when she sees her flowerbed!"

Chapter Four
Looking for Fun

It took Zoe and Nicola almost all afternoon to try and get the garden back to normal. Luckily, they were able to replant most of the flowers and they managed to sweep up all of the mud. While the girls worked, Max watched them from a lookout post on top of an upturned flowerpot. Every so often

he made a little peeping sound. Zoe
wondered what the sound meant but she
couldn't ask him with Nicola there!

"There, it's done," Zoe said, replanting
the last of the flowers.

"Phew," Nicola sighed, her face flushed.
"Living in a zoo might be fun but it's a
lot of hard work!"

Zoe laughed and nodded. "Let's go and
get some ice creams from the café to cool
down." She picked Max up and gave
him a cuddle. Max snuggled into her and
chattered happily. He really liked being
cuddled! Nicola was right, living in a
zoo could be hard work, but she wouldn't
change it for anything.

The next morning, Zoe got up early and
quickly made a new treasure-hunt banner

for the reptile house. On her way to drop off the banner she called by the meerkat enclosure. Max was standing guard on one of the logs. His mum and dad were both busy on the other side of the burrow, scrabbling about in the dirt with their front paws.

"What are they doing?" Zoe asked Mo.

"Foraging for food," Mo replied, "while Max takes care of his baby brother and sisters."

Zoe looked at Max. Every so often he made the same peeping sound he'd made when he'd been standing guard in the garden the day before. "Why's he making that noise?" she asked.

"It's to let the parents know that everything is OK," Mo said, heading out to check on the hippos. "So they don't have to worry while they're getting breakfast."

"I'm glad I don't have to forage for food," Meep chirped as Mo left. "It looks like hard work!"

Zoe laughed. Meep was right. Max's mum's and dad's front paws were moving very quickly and they were concentrating hard on finding food for their family. Then Zoe looked back at Max. He was still making the peeping sound but he'd got down from the log and was rolling around in the dirt – and the babies were

copying him. They looked so funny and cute. She felt for her paw-print pendant and let herself into the enclosure.

Max yelped and gave her a cheeky grin. Then he carried on wriggling around with his brother and sisters in the dirt.

All of a sudden their mum and dad came scampering over. Max's mum barked at him. She wanted to know why he'd stopped making the peeping sound. Max looked sad.

"Oh dear," Zoe whispered to Meep. "Max is in trouble again!"

While Max's mum and dad started grooming the babies Zoe put down her banner and gave Max a cuddle. He instantly looked happier and started chattering away to her.

"I know chores can be boring but everyone has to do them," Zoe said. "I have some jobs to do now for the treasure hunt. Why don't I ask Mo if I can take you out for a walk and I can show you what I'm doing?"

Max yelped excitedly.

When Mo had agreed that it was OK for her to take Max out, Zoe put Max on the lead and they set off around the zoo. Everywhere they went there were brightly coloured banners reminding visitors about the treasure hunt. Zoe's heart pounded with excitement – soon it would be time to hide the prizes. She couldn't wait! As they walked past the panda enclosure Chi Chi and Mei Mei came scampering over. They squealed with excitement when they saw Max on the lead.

The Messy Meerkat

"This is Max the meerkat," Zoe explained. "He's from Botswana in Africa. He's just moved to the zoo with his family."

The panda cubs gave Max a welcoming squeak. Max stood up tall on his hind legs, using his tail to support him, and said hello.

Finally they got to the reptile house. But when Max saw the monkey enclosure opposite he started tugging on his lead, trying to get closer. A couple of spider monkeys were playing a game of chase, hooting loudly as they swung from branch to branch. Max tugged even harder on his lead and yelped excitedly.

"No, you can't go in there," Zoe said. "But we can stay here and watch for a bit if you like."

Max hopped about happily.

Just then Sally, one of the reptile keepers, came out of the reptile house.

"Hello, Zoe," she called. "Do you have the banner for the treasure hunt?"

"Yes, hold on." Zoe crouched down next to Max and Meep. "You stay here and watch the monkeys," she whispered, before going over to Sally.

"Are you looking forward to the treasure hunt?" Sally asked, as Zoe handed her one end of the banner.

"I can't wait!" Zoe grinned. "I'm going to be helping hide the prizes tomorrow. We've got loads to hide *and* there's going to be a really cool special prize."

Zoe held her end of the banner straight while Sally unfurled it.

"Oh, Zoe, it looks amazing!" Sally exclaimed.

"Thank you!" Zoe said proudly. She'd covered the banner in paintings of lizards and it said: **TREASURE HUNT ON SATURDAY AT 11!** The S in Saturday was a huge snake. Zoe helped Sally attach it to the railings outside the reptile house, then they stepped back to look at it.

"Thanks so much, Zoe," Sally said. "Have fun hiding the prizes tomorrow!"

"I will," Zoe replied.

As Sally headed inside the reptile house, Zoe turned back to the monkey enclosure. But Max and Meep had disappeared!

Zoe ran over to the monkey enclosure and called to one of the spider monkeys. "Have you seen Meep and the little meerkat I was with?"

The monkey nodded and let out a shriek, pointing to the open door of the reptile house.

"Thank you!" Zoe hurried through the door of the reptile house and immediately bumped into Meep – a very worried-looking Meep.

"Meep, thank goodness! Where's Max?" Zoe exclaimed.

Meep raised one of his front paws. Zoe's heart sank as she realised that he was pointing straight to the snake room!

Zoe raced inside. As always the snake room was warm and dark. "Max?" she called softly.

A huge cobra slithered across the ground of one of the enclosures and gave a loud hiss. Zoe gulped. She didn't know

all of the snakes at the Rescue Zoo as
there were so many but normally they
were very polite. Why did this one sound
so cross? Surely Max wouldn't have been
silly enough to climb into his enclosure…
But then she saw a blur of pale-brown fur
streak across the back of the enclosure.
It was Max! She watched as the little

meerkat leapt on to the snake, chattering
excitedly.

"No, Max. You can't ride the snake!"
Zoe exclaimed.

The snake raised its head and gave
another loud hiss, its forked tongue
darting about. Then it flicked its long
body and sent Max tumbling to the floor.

"Max, come out of there right now," Zoe said crossly. "The snake doesn't want to play with you."

The snake looked at Zoe and hissed again.

"He wants to be left alone to have a nap," Zoe told Max. "I'm really sorry," she said to the snake. "He's new to the zoo!"

Max looked at Zoe and sighed. Then he scampered over to a tree at the back of the enclosure and shot up the branches. He leapt from the highest branch of the tree and out of a small gap at the top of the enclosure. Then he hopped straight down into Zoe's arms.

Inside the enclosure, the snake coiled back down with a contented hiss.

"What were you doing in there?" Zoe asked.

Max chirped in her ear.

"You were looking for fun – in an enclosure with a snake?" Zoe exclaimed.

Max nodded and smiled.

Zoe shook her head. She realised she couldn't leave the curious little meerkat on his own – not even for a minute!

Chapter Five
Chores are for Bores!

The next day was Friday – the day before the treasure hunt. Zoe woke up bright and early, feeling very excited.

"I wonder what funny things Max will do today," Meep said, hopping on to the bedroom windowsill.

"Hopefully nothing as dangerous as yesterday!" Zoe replied, as she put on her favourite tiger-print T-shirt. "We're lucky that the snake wasn't in a bad mood or he could have really hurt Max!" She turned round. "Meep, what are you doing?" The little lemur was standing upright with his tummy pressed against the window.

"I'm warming up like a meerkat," Meep replied.

"Oh, Meep," Zoe giggled. "I'm not sure if it works the same for mouse lemurs. Come on, let's get some breakfast."

Down in the kitchen, Lucy had placed a large cardboard box on the table.

"What's in the box?" Zoe asked.

"Prizes for the treasure hunt," Lucy smiled. "And here's the special prize." She took a bag from the kitchen counter and pulled out a huge cuddly meerkat toy.

"Oh, Mum, it's so cute!" Zoe exclaimed, stroking the meerkat's silky fur. "Whoever wins this is going to be so lucky."

"We'll have to hide all the prizes as soon as the zoo closes this evening," Lucy said, as she poured Zoe a glass of orange juice.

Zoe nodded eagerly. She couldn't wait!

After breakfast, Zoe and Meep headed for the meerkat enclosure. All of the other meerkats were in the centre of the enclosure but Max was standing on his own on the log, with his tummy facing the sun. As Zoe let herself into the enclosure Max's dad barked at him, asking him to help clean one of the tunnels. Max turned his head to one side, as if he hadn't heard.

"What are you doing, Max?" Zoe asked.

68

Max yelped at her.

"But surely you must be warm enough by now," Zoe replied. "The sun's been up for ages." She bit on her lip to try and stop herself from grinning. She thought she knew what was really going on. "Is it because you don't want to help clean the tunnel?" she whispered, crouching down next to him.

Max nodded and chirped in her ear.

"What did he say?" Meep asked.

"He said chores are for bores," Zoe replied.

Meep giggled and Zoe had to turn away to hide her smile from Max. He was right, chores could be boring, but she really didn't want him getting into trouble with his mum and dad again. How could she show him that jobs had to be done ... and that they didn't have to be super boring?

"I know," she said. "If you go and clean the tunnel, I'll show you the chores I have to do and how I make them more fun."

Max nodded, then he bounded down from the log over to his mum and dad and started cleaning the tunnel.

"But you don't always enjoy your jobs, Zoe!" Meep chirped.

"You're right," Zoe replied. "But helping other people sometimes is important. We just have to show Max that, and it will hopefully make him feel better about the jobs he has to do!"

Once Max had cleaned the tunnel and Zoe had checked with Mo that it was OK for her to take Max out of his enclosure, the three friends set off into the zoo.

The first chore Zoe had to do was
help Kieran the kangaroo keeper
sweep out the part of the enclosure
where the kangaroos slept, including
Bouncer the baby kangaroo. Zoe tied
Max's lead to a post and began sweeping
away the old straw.

Max chattered curiously.

"I'm making it nice and clean," Zoe
explained. After she finished sweeping, she
went and fetched some fresh straw.

Max yawned.

"It might look boring but this will make
it all cosy for the kangaroos tonight," Zoe
explained. "It feels nice doing something
to help them."

Max turned round and round in circles,
chasing his tail.

Zoe frowned. She wasn't sure her plan

was working yet! Next she had to deliver
more leaflets about the hunt to the café
– perhaps Max would find that more
interesting. She untied Max's lead from
the post and led him out of the enclosure.

Outside the café the tables were bustling
with visitors sipping cool drinks and
eating ice creams in the sun. When they
saw Zoe approaching with Max and
Meep, they started pointing and smiling.
Zoe took her leaflets from her bag and
started handing them out.

"There's going to be a treasure hunt
here tomorrow," she told the visitors. "It'll
be so much fun."

"What a lovely idea," a lady said as
she looked at the leaflet. "I'll bring my
grandchildren along!"

Zoe beamed with pride. Max looked

happy too, exploring and getting lots of
attention from everyone!

Once Zoe had given out her leaflets she set off back to the cottage. It was time to show Max some of the chores she had to do at home.

When they got to the cottage Zoe went straight to the cupboard under the stairs and got out the vacuum cleaner. She helped her mum to vacuum each week and she quite enjoyed that job. She hoped Max would think it was fun too! She switched the vacuum on and started to clean.

Max began barking really loudly.

Zoe turned off the vacuum cleaner. Max kept on barking. "Max, what's wrong?"

"He's doing his warning bark," Meep said.

Zoe giggled. "Oh no, Max, the vacuum

cleaner isn't going to hurt you! It cleans dirt off the carpet."

Max kept barking at the vacuum cleaner suspiciously and so Zoe put it away again.

"Let's go into the kitchen," Zoe said. "I'll show you some of the things I do to help there."

They all went into the kitchen. Max started barking excitedly when he saw the huge toy meerkat on the table.

"No, it's not a real meerkat," Zoe laughed. "It's a toy for people to play with."

Max barked again.

"No, you can't play with it. It's the special prize for the treasure hunt tomorrow. Anyway, I need to get on with another one of the jobs." Zoe opened the

dishwasher and started to load it with the plates from breakfast.

"This is how we get everything clean," Zoe said. "And I – uh – make it fun by singing the cleaning dishes song."

Zoe quickly tried to think of a song about doing the dishes.

"*Hip, hip hooray! It's dish cleaning day!*"

she sang.

Meep giggled loudly.

"*One of my greatest wishes, is for sparkly, shiny dishes.*" Zoe looked at Max hopefully. He was perched on the counter staring at her. He barked loudly.

"Why does the machine clean the dishes?" Zoe said.

Max nodded.

"Well, it makes our bowls and plates nice and clean so that we can use them again for different food, later."

Max barked again.

Zoe burst out laughing. "No, Max! We can't lick them clean!"

"Why not?" Meep asked. "I always lick my bowl clean."

Zoe sighed. This wasn't working as well as she had hoped!

Max leapt down from the counter and

scampered out of the room, with Meep chasing after him.

Zoe finished loading the dishwasher and then followed them into her bedroom. Max was standing upright on her bedside cabinet, with his tummy facing the lamp. Meep was hopping up and down, hooting with laughter.

"Look, Zoe, he's warming up!" the little mouse lemur cried.

Zoe started to laugh. He might not have been enjoying Zoe's chores ... but at least Max was having some fun!

Chapter Six
Hiding the Treasure

After lunch, Zoe took Max back to his
enclosure. Lots of visitors had gathered
around to see the newest arrivals at the
Rescue Zoo. Great-Uncle Horace was
there too, telling them all about the
meerkats in the wild.

"Oh, look at that meerkat on a lead!" a
boy cried when he saw Zoe.

"Aha, Zoe!" Great-Uncle Horace exclaimed. "How's this little fellow doing?" He bent down and peered over his glasses at Max.

"He's doing really well," Zoe said. "He loves going out for walks and meeting people."

Max's mum yelped when she saw Max, and his dad barked some instructions to him. They wanted Max to help groom the

babies. Zoe let herself into the enclosure
and carefully removed Max's lead.

"Grooming your baby brother and
sisters is a really nice thing to do," she
whispered hopefully in his ear.

Max tilted his head to one side, like he
was thinking hard. Then he nodded and
scampered off to the babies.

"As you can see, meerkat families work very closely together to take care of each other," Great-Uncle Horace told the crowd.

Zoe watched as Max's mum and dad got busy on the other side of the enclosure, foraging for food. She couldn't believe how fast their paws moved. Then she heard laughter coming from outside the enclosure. She turned to see several of the visitors giggling and pointing. Zoe looked over at Max.

"Oh no!" she exclaimed.

Instead of grooming the young meerkats, Max and the babies were rolling around in the dirt! And now, instead of one messy meerkat, there were four! Zoe's heart sank. Max's mum and dad had stopped foraging and were

looking around to see what was causing
the commotion. When they saw Max
and the babies rolling about in the dirt
they came scampering over.

Max's dad barked crossly at him. Then
he and Max's mum set about grooming
the dirt from the babies' fur. Max slunk
off to a corner of the enclosure looking
very grumpy. Zoe sighed. Would Max *ever*
enjoy helping out his family?

Once the zoo was closed for the evening
Zoe and Lucy took the prizes for the
treasure hunt and went and met up with
the zookeepers outside the café.

"Here are the prizes to hide around
your enclosure," Zoe said, handing each
of the zookeepers a bag of treats. "And
here are the answers to the clues to show

you where to hide them." She handed them each a sheet of instructions. She'd had a lot of fun writing out rhyming clues for each of the hiding places.

"Oh, who's going to hide the special prize?" Zoe asked Lucy, pulling the cuddly meerkat from the bag. The night before, she'd attached a large gold bow and a sign saying SPECIAL PRIZE to its packaging.

"I think you should do it," Lucy told her. "The treasure hunt was your idea, after all."

"Cool!" Zoe knew exactly where she was going to hide the prize. It had to be near the new meerkat enclosure!

"OK then, happy hiding, everyone!" Lucy called.

As the zookeepers all headed off to their

enclosures, Zoe and Meep hurried over to the meerkats. When they got there Zoe saw Max standing by the enclosure wall, gazing out. When he saw Zoe his ears pricked up and he yelped excitedly.

"Sorry, I can't take you for a walk," Zoe said. "I have to hide this special prize." She showed him the cuddly meerkat.

Max yelped again.

"No, you still can't play with him, I'm afraid." Zoe spotted the perfect hiding place for the toy, a nearby bush with bright green leaves.

"Ooh, good idea," Zoe hurried over to the bush and crouched down. Then she parted the branches and placed the toy meerkat deep inside.

Max watched her closely.

Then Zoe saw Mr Pinch heading

towards her.

"Hello, Mr Pinch," she called. "I'm just hiding the special prize for the treasure hunt."

"Hmm, well, I hope *you're* going to tidy up the mess that gets made tomorrow," Mr Pinch said with a frown.

"I will," Zoe replied. "It's going to be such a fun day!"

Mr Pinch sighed. "I don't call all this fuss and nonsense fun," he muttered crossly, before turning and marching away.

Zoe stuck her tongue out at his back. Mr Pinch might be the grumpiest person ever, but nothing could spoil the special treasure hunt!

Chapter Seven
Another Messy Meerkat

Zoe was woken up early the next morning by the sound of the elephants trumpeting and the monkeys chattering. It turned out she wasn't the only one excited about the treasure hunt – the animals couldn't wait too!

"Hip-hip hooray, it's finding treasure day!" Meep chirped as he bounced up and down on the end of Zoe's bed.

Zoe giggled and quickly got dressed. She and her mum still had some last-minute clues to put around the zoo before it opened. With Meep on her shoulder she hurried downstairs.

In the kitchen, Lucy was making blueberry pancakes. She'd also put some of the blueberries in a bowl with some seeds for Meep. The little mouse lemur gobbled them up hungrily.

"I can't wait for the treasure hunt to begin," Zoe said excitedly. "I hope the person who wins the special prize likes meerkats."

"I'm sure they will," Lucy said as she flipped a pancake over.

Just then there was a knock on the door.

"Do I smell pancakes?" a voice boomed

through the letterbox.

"Great-Uncle Horace!" Zoe rushed to open the door. "It's treasure-hunt day!"

"I know," Great-Uncle Horace said, giving Zoe a big hug. "Kiki and I are most excited." Kiki fluttered down from his shoulder and perched on the top of the kitchen cupboard. "You've done a wonderful job of arranging all this, Lucy and Zoe."

"Thank you. But we haven't finished yet," Zoe said, sitting down at the table. "We still have some clues to put up."

"Would you like to help us, Uncle Horace?" Lucy asked.

"I most certainly would." Great-Uncle Horace gave her a twinkly-eyed grin. "As long as you give me some of your delicious pancakes. Putting up clues is hungry work!"

As soon as they finished breakfast, Zoe, Lucy and Great-Uncle Horace headed out into the zoo with the clues. Zoe had written them in gold on brightly coloured card. Lucy went off to put some clues by the zoo hospital, and Zoe and Great-Uncle Horace made their way to the panda enclosure. When Mei Mei and Chi Chi saw Great-Uncle Horace they scampered over and gave excited squeals. All of the animals at the Rescue Zoo loved Great-Uncle Horace and were very grateful to him for saving them and giving them such a lovely home.

"Goodness me, look how big you've got!" Great-Uncle Horace exclaimed. When he first brought the pandas to the zoo they'd been small cubs.

Chi Chi and Mei Mei squealed again.
Zoe knew that they were saying thank
you to Great-Uncle Horace! Once they'd
put out some of the clues, they moved on
to the penguin enclosure. Zoe had chosen
blue and white bunting to match the blue
of the lagoon and the giant glittering
iceberg. As soon as the penguins
saw Great-Uncle Horace

they dived off the iceberg and swam over.
    "Look, they're so excited to see you."
Zoe smiled.

"And I'm excited to see them too," Great-Uncle Horace replied, adjusting his round glasses and peering into the lagoon. The penguins flapped their wings joyfully as they greeted Great-Uncle Horace.

Finally, after putting up clues by the lion enclosure and the insect house, they just had one left.

"Let's put it by the meerkat enclosure," Zoe said. She wanted to check how Max was doing.

"Excellent plan!" Great-Uncle Horace replied.

As they walked past the hippo enclosure the sun was just coming up over the lake. Zoe smiled, imagining the meerkats warming up on a log.

But when they got to the enclosure the meerkats were nowhere to be seen.

Then Zoe heard an urgent barking from the other side of the enclosure. She hurried round to investigate and found Max's mum and dad by a freshly dug hole right next to the glass wall. The three babies were huddled together by a nearby log. There was no sign of Max.

"Goodness me, what's all the commotion

about?" Great-Uncle Horace exclaimed.

"I'm not sure," Zoe replied, but she had a horrible feeling Max had something to do with it.

"What on earth is making that dreadful racket?" Mr Pinch said as he marched down the footpath towards them. As usual, his uniform was extra smart and his polished shoes gleamed in the morning sunlight.

"Good morning, Mr Pinch," Great-Uncle Horace said cheerily. "Yes, the meerkats are certainly full of beans this morning. They must be excited for the treasure hunt."

"They're not the only ones," Mr Pinch said. "There's a huge queue of people outside waiting to get in." To Zoe's surprise he actually smiled. "That's one good thing about the treasure hunt, I suppose. More money for the zoo. I'd better go and open the gates." He walked on briskly.

In the enclosure, Max's mum and dad carried on barking.

Zoe wondered what was wrong.

Then she heard Mr Pinch yelling. "This is NOT acceptable!" She turned and saw him standing by the bush where she'd hidden the special prize the night before.

"What on earth's the matter?" Great-Uncle Horace asked as he and Zoe hurried over.

"Uh-oh!" Meep exclaimed, scampering along ahead of them.

"Oh no!" Zoe said when she saw the reason why Mr Pinch was so cross.

There, next to the bush, was a freshly

dug hole and a big pile of mud and dirt.
And next to the hole was a very muddy,
messy Max. A golden bow lay on the
ground beside him, next to the SPECIAL
PRIZE sign and torn strips of wrapping
paper. And there was Max, holding the
cuddly toy meerkat, which was also
totally covered in mud.

"What is the meaning of this?" Mr
Pinch spluttered.

"What's going on?" Mo asked, running
up the path to join them.

"It looks as if someone dug an escape
tunnel," Great-Uncle Horace chuckled.

"Oh no!" Mo groaned. "There must
be a weak spot in the foundation of the
enclosure wall. I'll have to find it and fix
it." He hurried off to the enclosure.

"What's he's holding?" Great-Uncle

Horace said, pointing to Max.

"It's the special prize," Zoe cried. "He's made a mess of the special treasure-hunt prize!"

"Oh dear!" Great-Uncle Horace said,

shaking his head.

"I'm about to open the zoo," Mr Pinch
spluttered, looking down at the muddy,
messy meerkats. "We can't have animals
escaping all over the place! And what
about this mess?"

"Don't worry, Percy," Great-Uncle
Horace replied. "We'll have him back
in his enclosure in no time and we'll get
everything looking spick and span."

"But what about the special prize?"
Zoe said glumly as Mr Pinch strolled
off, muttering and shaking his head. Zoe
went over to Max and took the toy from
him. "Everyone's going to be searching
for the special prize in the treasure hunt.
But we can't give it away now, it's filthy!"

When Max saw how sad Zoe was he
hung his head and yelped.

Zoe stroked him. She knew that he'd only wanted to play with the toy meerkat, but the special prize was ruined! What was she going to do? The cuddly meerkat had been the best gift ever. Unless... Zoe suddenly had a great idea.

"What if we changed the special prize?" Zoe said to Great-Uncle Horace. "What if instead of a cuddly meerkat the prize was to *cuddle* a meerkat? Max loves being held and stroked. I'm sure he'd really enjoy that."

"That sounds like a great idea!" Great-Uncle Horace smiled. He called Mo over and asked him what he thought. Zoe whispered her suggestion to Max who nodded his little head, eager to make up for his naughty behaviour. Mo also agreed that it was a brilliant plan and went back to carefully checking the enclosure.

Great-Uncle Horace took a pen from his jacket pocket. He picked up the special prize sign and wrote on the back in big, fancy letters:

Congratulations! You have won the special prize of cuddling a meerkat!

Then Great-Uncle Horace tucked the piece of card and the bow back under the bush.

"Good thinking, Zoe," he said, patting her on the back. "Now, let's get this little chap back inside his enclosure."

Zoe picked up Max and they turned back to the enclosure, but just then Mo came running towards them. He looked really worried.

"Mo, what on earth is the matter?"

Great-Uncle Horace asked.

"It's the baby meerkats," Mo said. "They've escaped too!"

Chapter Eight
The Baby Meerkat Hunt

Zoe looked at Mo in shock. "How have they escaped?"

"I'm guessing the same way this little fellow did," Great-Uncle Horace said, pointing at Max. "Through the tunnel."

Max looked really upset.

"Oh no!" Zoe looked around for any sign of the baby meerkats but they were nowhere to be seen.

Max yelped to Zoe. She cuddled him close to her and whispered in his ear. "It's OK, I know you didn't mean for them to copy you."

"We need to find them quickly," Mo said. "Look, the visitors are arriving and soon the zoo will be packed!"

Zoe looked over to the zoo gates in the distance. A stream of people were making their way into the zoo, all clutching their treasure maps.

"Let's split up," Great-Uncle Horace said. "That way we can search quicker."

"OK, I'll go this way," Zoe said, heading off down the path towards the hippo enclosure with Max in her arms and Meep scampering after her.

Max chattered anxiously to Zoe.

"I really hope they're OK too," Zoe replied.

When they got to the hippo enclosure, Henry came lumbering over to greet them.

"Have you seen any baby meerkats?" Zoe asked him. "They've escaped from their enclosure."

Henry shook his head and grunted.

"OK, let's try the monkeys." Zoe hurried off along the path. In the distance she could see the crowds of visitors running this way and that, beginning their search for treasure. She bit her lip. When she'd hidden the prizes for the treasure hunt she thought she was going to be able to have fun watching people find them. She had no idea she'd be going on her own hunt – for baby meerkats!

When they got to
the monkey enclosure
Zoe called out to a
marmoset named
Maisie. "Maisie,
have you seen
any baby
meerkats go by?"
Maisie shook
her head. Then
she hooted
to Zoe and
scampered up
into the branches
of a tall tree.
"She's going
to see if she
can see them
from up there

where she'll have a better view," Zoe explained to Max and Meep.

When Maisie got to the very top of the tree she looked all around. Then she swung back down through the branches and scampered over to Zoe, chattering and shaking her head sadly.

"Thanks for trying!" Zoe called. She looked around. The paths were now full of people. Over by the reptile house a little girl gave a shriek of delight as she grabbed a packet of sweets from behind the banner. "Mummy, look, I've found some treasure!"

Zoe, Meep and Max carried on up the path. Max started yelping loudly when he saw the reptile house.

Zoe stared at him. "Why do you think the baby meerkats are in there?"

Max barked sheepishly.

"You told them that you had a brilliant time riding on the snake?" Zoe cried. "But that's not true, Max! The snake was very cross and you were lucky not to get hurt. What happens if the babies get into trouble?"

Max looked really worried.

"Come on, there's no time to waste." Zoe hurried inside the reptile house with Max and Meep close behind her.

Thankfully there were no visitors in the snake room. Zoe squinted in the darkness. It was hard to see anything after the brightness of the sun. In the enclosure closest to them a huge cobra was uncoiling.

Max leapt out of Zoe's arms and clambered on top of an information sign.

He stood up straight and threw back his head and started barking really loudly. Zoe realised he was giving the warning bark. She held her breath. Surely if the babies were nearby they'd come running when they heard him. She and Meep stood still and waited as Max continued to bark. Moments later Zoe heard the scampering of paws on the floor and she turned to see the babies hurrying out from a darkened corner of the cobra enclosure!

Zoe rushed over and carefully lifted each of the baby meerkats out of the enclosure. They looked a bit frightened and were very relieved to see their big brother.

The babies huddled close to Max and he began chattering away to them. Zoe realised the babies were telling Max that they thought they'd ask the big cobra if they could have a ride on him. But when he uncoiled they realised just how big he was and they felt very scared. So they had stayed very still in the corner of the enclosure. Max was telling them to stay away from all snakes in future, as they could be very dangerous.

"I think Max might have learned his lesson," Meep chattered, and Zoe smiled with relief. She knew the baby meerkats could have been in *big* trouble if the cobra had spotted them and been feeling hungry…

"OK, we need to get you back to your mum and dad," she said, crouching down by the meerkats.

Max yelped excitedly.

"You want to lead them home?" Zoe said.

Max nodded.

Zoe thought for a moment. Could Max be trusted to look after his brother and sisters?

She knelt down next to Max. "Do you promise you'll stay close to me and lead them straight back to the enclosure?"

Max nodded his head and stood up even taller. Then he barked at the babies and they all got into a line.

Zoe smiled. Max certainly *seemed* to be taking his job as big brother seriously.

"OK then, follow me," she said.

Meep hopped up on to her shoulder and Zoe led the meerkats out of the reptile house. Outside, the paths were busier than ever with people searching for treasure. But as soon as they saw Zoe and the line of meerkats behind her they stopped and smiled.

"Ah, look at those meerkats!" a little girl exclaimed.

Max puffed his chest up proudly and checked that his baby brother and sisters were OK.

They carried on walking along the winding footpath, back past the monkey enclosure. Maisie shrieked excitedly when she saw the babies. Then they walked past the hippos. Henry tilted his huge head back and grunted happily when he saw them. All around them the visitors stopped

searching for treasure and pointed
and giggled at the meerkat procession.
But, as he'd promised, Max didn't get
distracted and stayed close to his baby
siblings. Finally they arrived back at the
meerkat enclosure. Zoe used her paw-
print pendant to open the gate and Max
marched the babies inside. His mum
and dad came scampering over, barking
excitedly.

Zoe crouched down beside them as
Max told them that he was really sorry
and promised he'd never mess around
again.

Zoe couldn't help giggling at how
serious he'd become. Max's mum and
dad groomed him affectionately and
chattered away. Zoe smiled. They were
telling him that it was OK to mess around

and have fun sometimes – just not all the time. And that *all* the meerkats should stay away from snakes!

"Zoe, you found them. Thank goodness!" Zoe turned to see Great-Uncle Horace and Mo entering the enclosure.

"Yes. Well, Max found them really," Zoe said with a smile, stroking Max on the head.

"What a relief," Mo exclaimed. "I've fixed the enclosure wall, so it definitely won't happen again."

Just then there was a shout from outside. Zoe turned to see a little girl jumping up and down by the bush.

"I've found the special prize!" she exclaimed, waving the card around. "I'm going to cuddle a meerkat!"

"Aha, we have a winner," Great-Uncle

Horace said to Zoe, his eyes twinkling. "Would you like to give the young lady her prize?"

Zoe nodded. Then she picked Max up. The little meerkat looked very sad.

"What's the matter?" Zoe asked as she headed over to the gate of the enclosure.

He chattered sadly in her ear.

"Oh, you haven't ruined the prize," Zoe whispered. "You *are* the prize. This little girl wants to give you a cuddle!" Zoe pointed to the girl, who was still jumping up and down with excitement.

Max barked happily.

Zoe took him out of the enclosure and over to the girl. She showed her how to sit still and let Max sit on her lap.

"This is Max," she said. "He's a very important member of our new meerkat family. He's the baby meerkats' big brother."

Max nodded importantly.

As Max settled down happily Zoe and Mo told the little girl all about meerkats and their special skills.

"Thank you," the little girl said, stroking Max softly. "This is the best prize *ever*!"

Later, once the treasure hunt was over
and all the visitors had gone, Zoe began
making her way back to the cottage.
The setting sun was dipping
down behind the trees in the
giraffe enclosure, making
the zoo shine in the
evening sun. *What
a lovely day!* Zoe
thought to herself as
she skipped along
beside Meep.

The treasure hunt had been a huge success, Max had learned an important lesson *and* he'd rescued the baby meerkats.

As she opened the door of the cottage her mum greeted her with a huge smile. "I have a special something for you," she said, sounding very pleased with herself.

"What is it?" Zoe asked.

"A special prize for all of your hard work with the treasure hunt." Lucy handed her a present, wrapped in gold paper.

Zoe opened it excitedly. She nearly dropped it in surprise when she saw the toy meerkat inside! Its fur was now fluffy and clean and it looked as good as new. "The cuddly meerkat!" she exclaimed. "But how did it get so clean?"

"I popped it in the washing machine,"

Lucy said with a grin.

"Thank you!" Zoe hugged the toy meerkat to her and then hugged her mum. Just when she'd thought the day couldn't get any better, *she'd* won a very special prize that she'd treasure forever!

Zoe's Rescue Zoo

Look out for more amazing animal adventures at the Rescue Zoo!

The Secret Rescuers

If you enjoyed this book,
we think you'll love The Secret Rescuers!

The Rescue Princesses

Look out for another AMAZING series from Nosy Crow!

Friendship, animals and
secret royal adventures!